Where Hummingbirds Come From
Bilingual Nepali - English

Copyright © 2010 - by Adele Marie Crouch

www.creationsbycrouch.com

Thank you to my wonderful husband, Doug, for his patience throughout the years with my late
night writing habits and eccentric ways. A special note of gratitude to my daughter, Charlie, for
insisting I could do this. And thank you to everyone who read *How The Fox Got His Color* and
Where Hummingbirds Come From and enjoyed them, prior to publication.

It was a cold winter day. The snow was falling outside and Grandmother was in her chair by the fireplace.

एकदम जाडो दिन थियो. बाहिर हिउँ जराकोथ्यो, हजुरामा कुर्शी मा बस्नु भकियोथ्यो

एकदमै जाडोको दिन थियो. बाहिर हिउ परिरहेको थियो, हजुरआमा आगोको नजिक आफ्नो कुर्सीमा बस्नुभएको थियो.

She had that far away look she gets sometimes. I crawled up into her lap hoping for a story.

बेलाबेलामा उसमा अति दुरसम्मको हेराई झल्कन्थियो. म हजुरआमाको काखमा गएर कथा सुन्नको लागि तयार भएर बसे.

She wrapped her arms around me and said, "When I was a little girl just like you, my Grandmother told me about some magic waters."

उसले मलाई उस्को दुवै हाथले लपेट्दै भन्नुभयो, " जब म तिमी जस्तै सानो थिए, मेरो हजुरआमाले मलाई जादूवाला पानीहरुकोबारेमा बताउनुभयो."

Grandmother smiled at me and asked, "Would you like to hear what she had to say?"

हजुरआमा मतिर हेरेर हास्दै सोध्नुभयो," तिमीलाई पनि सुन्नु मन छ उसले के भनेको थियो?"

Oh boy, I thought, as I eagerly shook my head yes. *This is just what I was hoping for.*

"ओह बोय!" मलाई लाग्यो, कि मैले धेरै उत्सुकसाथ हुन्छ भनि टाउको हल्लाए. "यहि नै मेरो इच्छा पनि थियो."

This is the way my Grandmother told me.....

यसरी मेरो हजुरआमाले मलाई भन्नुभएको थियो.........

"It was the time of the new beginning, when the leaves bust open on the trees, and flowers start to blossom. In a meadow, up in the mountains, near the cabin where I was born, a babbling brook appeared out of nowhere.

"यो नयाँ समयको सुरुवात थियो, जब रुखमा नयाँ पातहरु पलाउन लागेका थिए, फुलहरु फुल्न लागेका थिए." हजुरआमाले बताउनुभयो. " घाँस भएको, माथी पहाडमा, सानु कूटियामा जहाँ मेरो जन्म भएको थियो, कहीबाट सानो खोला देखापर्यो."

The water was fresh, and clear, and sweet, like nectar.

त्यहाको पानी एकदमै शुद्ध, सफा अनि अमृत जस्तै मिठो थियो.

Then, it flowed across the meadow, where it cascaded over rocks. And then, as soon as it began to bounce across the rocks, the water glistened with the fabulous colors of nature."

"त्यसपछि," वहाँले भन्नुभयो, "यो घाँसभुमिको वारपार बगिरहेको थियो, जहाँ यो ढुंगाको माथिबाट

झरना भई बगेको थियो, भनि हजुरआमाले भन्नुभयो, "त्यसपछि मेरो हजुरआमाको भनाई अनुसार, यो जति सक्दो चाडो ढुंगामा ठोकक्यो, उतिनै राम्रो रंगमा यो पानी प्रकृतिमा चम्म्केको देखिन्थियो."

Grandmother's voice was almost a whisper as she went on to say, "Then, the water began to sing and a breeze started to blow very soft and gentle.

हजुरआमा एकदमै कानेखुसीको आवाज गरेर भन्नुभयो, " त्यसपछि पानीले गीत गाउनलागे अनि हल्का हावाको तेजले बिस्तारै ति लहरलाई उडाउन लाग्यो."

As the breeze hit the magic waters, it lifted a dainty mist into the air. In the mist were all the colors in the rainbow as the sun sparkled off the spray of water."

"जब मन्द हावाको तेजले त्यो जादुवाला पानीलाई छुन्थियो, तब बिस्तारै ति सुक्ष्म पानीका बाफहरू हावामा उद्थे. हजुरआमाले भन्नुभयो, ती बाफ़मा, घामको किरणले गर्दा इन्द्रेनीका सबै रंगहरु छरिएको देखिन्थियो.

"Suddenly!" Grandmother said, with a gleam in her eye. "From the song of the magic waters, and the colors of the rainbow, the mist became hummingbirds."

"अचानक!" हजुरआमाले आखाँमा थोरै चमक लाएर भन्नुभयो, " जादुवाला पानीको गीत, अनि इन्द्रेणीको रंगबाट निस्केको पानीको बाफबाट हुम्मिंग चरा बन्नगयो.

"My Grandmother told me, just as I am telling you, this is what happened next. They spread their wings, did flips in the air, fanned out their tails, and even flew backward!"

"मेरो हजुरआमाले भन्नुभयो, ठिक जसरी म तिमीलाई बताउदैछु, त्यसरी नै अब अगाडी के भएको थियो भनेर. उनीहरुले आफ्ना प्वाखहरु फैलाउदै, हावामा जोडसंग फ्याटफ्याट गर्‍यो, पुच्छर बाहिर फैलाउदै, उनीहरुले उल्टोबाट उस्तै तरिकाले उड़े!"

Grandmother spread out her arms and with a big smile on her face and exclaimed, "What great fun they were having dancing in the sun!"

हजुरआमाले आफ्नो हातहरु फैलाउदै अनि ठुलो हाँसो मुखमा ल्याउदै, सम्झाउनुभयो, "उनीहरु एकदमै आनन्दका साथ घाममा नाचिरहेका थिए!"

"Swooping and twirling they fanned out across the meadow. They fluttered over the flowers, putting their tiny beaks in each one, taking a taste of the nectar as they went from one to the next.

"एक्कासि उनीहरुले घाँसभूमिको वारपार घुम्दै हावा लगाउनथाले." उनीहरु फूलहरुको माथि फड फडाउन लागे, आफ्नो सानो चुच्चोहरु हरेक फुलमा हाल्दै त्यसको पुष्परस चाख्दै एकबाट अर्कोमा गए भनि हजुरआमाले सम्झाउनुभयो.

They liked the red flowers the best, or so it seemed. This is the reason people put red coloring in their hummingbird feeders. At least that is what my grandmother said.

"उनीहरुलाई रातो फुलहरु सबैभन्दा राम्रो लाग्थियो, अथवा त्यस्तै आभास हुन्थियो. यहि कारणले गर्दा मानिसहरुले हुम्मिंग चारको चारोदानीहरु रातोरंग लगाएका थिए. कमसेकम त्यसैले होला मेरो हजुरआमाले भन्नेगर्नु हुन्थियो."

"This magic continued through the 9th day of April, making hummingbirds of all colors. Have you ever noticed," Grandmother asked "that the hummingbird's colors shimmer like the sun reflecting off of a raindrop?"

"यो जादु लगातार अप्रिलको नौ दिन सम्म चल्यो." हुम्मिंग चरालाई सबै रंग बनाउनलाई. "के तिमीले कहिले याद गरेका छौ" भनेर हजुरआमाले सोध्नुभयो, पानीको थोपा हुम्मिंग चराको रंगमा परेको बेला

घामको किरण पर्‍यो भने चम्म्किनछ?.

"At the end of the day, on the 9th of April, the magic water quietly went back into the ground. I wonder," Grandmother said, with a quizzical look on her face, "If my Grandmother's story has the magic water disappear on April 9th, because it is my birthday?

"त्यो दिनको अन्त, नौ अप्रिलको दिन त्यो जादुवाला पानी चुपचापसंग जमिनमुनि गयो. आश्चर्यका साथ हजुरआमाले भन्नुभयो, अजिबकिसिमको अनुहार लगाउदै, " यदि मेरो हजुरआमाको जादुवाला पानीको कथा अप्रिल नौमा हरायो किनभने आज मेरो जन्मदिन हो?"

"Anyway, on with the story, she said with a smile as she hugged me tightly, "This is how we have the hummingbird.

"जे भएपनि, यो कथा अनुसार," वहाँले हाँस्दै मलाई कसेर अंगालो हाल्दै भन्नुभयो, " यसरी हम्मिंग चरा आज हामीसंग छ."

"These tiny, lovely birds come back every year. Flittering from flower to flower, dancing in the sky, and putting on a show for anyone who cares to watch.

यी साना, राम्रा चराहरु हरेक साल यहाँ आउञ्छन. उनीहरु एकफुलबाट अर्को फुलमा उड्दै आकाशमा नाच्दै, प्रदर्शन देखाऊछन् यदि कोहि हेर्नलाई इच्छुक भए."

Now then, my Grandmother told me, the hummingbird is a symbol of love and happiness." Grandmother gave me a big kiss on the cheek and said, "So I am passing this love and happiness on to you!"

"त्यसपछि मेरो हजुरआमाले भन्नुभयो, हम्मिंग चराहरु प्यार र खुशीका प्रतिक हुन्." त्यसैले म तिमीलाई मेरो प्यार अनि खुशी बाइदैछु.

As I have grown older, I've noticed the hummingbirds begin to appear in my yard every year right around my grandmother's birthday.
I wonder................... Is April 9th a magic day?

जबजब म ठुलो हुन्दैगये, मरो ध्यानमा आयो कि मेरो हजुरआमाको जन्मदिनको समयमा हरेक साल हम्मिंग चराहरु हाम्रो घरको बगैचामा देखिन्छन्. मलाई आश्चर्य लाग्छ............के अप्रिल नौ सच्चि कै जादुवाला दिन हो?

About the Author

Adele is an artist as well as a published author. Her books are currently available on Amazon and through her web site (http://www.creationsbycrouch.com).

Creations by Crouch is making an attempt to produce bilingual books that will not only assist people in learning the language of their choice, but also to preserve (in some small way) languages that are in danger of becoming extinct. With that in mind, Adele is always on the lookout for translators of new and endangered languages. Please feel free to contact Adele if you are a native speaker of any Native American languages.

"Alphabet Alliteration" is a new twist on an old subject, learning the English alphabet. "How The Fox Got His Color" and "Where Hummingbirds Come From" are picture books for children ages 3 - 6 years of age. "The Dance of The Caterpillars", a lesson in prepositions is designed for 2nd grade students. "The Gnomes of Knot-Hole Manor" is a chapter book targeting 3rd graders. It teaches words with silent letters and words that sound the same but are spelled differently.

"Catherine's Travels" is an historic novel that takes place in Missouri during the 1800's. Catherine and her family flee war torn Austria seeking a new life in America. Disaster strikes and Catherine finds herself alone in the wilderness.

"Catherine's Travels Book 2 ~ Lawson's Search" After Lawson's beautiful wife, Catherine, is kidnapped he embarks on a search that will take him across the United States, over the Rocky Mountains and into the land of the Navajo. Catherine will take a terrifying, yet rewarding journey with her husband's archenemy. Blue Eyes goes on a vision quest that will change his life forever.

Adele's children's books have become popular with English as a second language students and foreign language students all over the world and are on the top 10 list of ESL study material on Amazon. Her website is filled with study material to help people study foreign languages. It includes - vocabulary lists, MP3 files, and even has a list of the questions you need to know to pass the US citizenship exam. All of this is free to the viewer. See: www.creationsbycrouch.com

If you wish to contact Adele, you can email: Adele@creationsbycrouch.com

Alphabet Alliteration

अक्षर को अनुप्रास

Bilingual Nepali-English

C c

Written and Illustrated by:
Adele Marie Crouch
Translated by:
Richa Pokhrel

How the Fox Got His Color

Bilingual Nepali - English

फ्याउरोले कसरी उसको रंग पायो

Illustrated by
Megan Gibbs

Written by
Adele Marie
Crouch

Translated by
Richa Pokhrel

The Dance of the Caterpillars

Bilingual Nepali - English

झुस्लेकीराहरु को नाच

Written and Illustrated by:
Adele Marie Crouch

Translated by:
Richa Pokhrel

CPSIA information can be obtained at www.ICGtesting.com
Printed in the USA
LVIW01n2158120415
434312LV00004B/7